c.1

E
KRA   Kraus, Robert

           Strudwick

DUE DATE	BRODART	11/95	14.99
5/21/98			
10/3/00			
12/2/02			

34698000062282

STRUDWICK

A Sheep in Wolf's Clothing

ROBERT KRAUS

VIKING

VIKING
Published by the Penguin Group
Penguin Books USA Inc., 375 Hudson Street, New York, New York 10014, U.S.A.
Penguin Books Ltd, 27 Wrights Lane, London W8 5TZ, England
Penguin Books Australia Ltd, Ringwood, Victoria, Australia
Penguin Books Canada Ltd, 10 Alcorn Avenue, Toronto, Ontario, Canada M4V 3B2
Penguin Books (N.Z.) Ltd, 182-190 Wairau Road, Auckland 10, New Zealand

Penguin Books Ltd, Registered Offices: Harmondsworth, Middlesex, England

First published in 1995 by Viking, a division of Penguin Books USA Inc.

1   3   5   7   9   10   8   6   4   2

LIBRARY OF CONGRESS CATALOGING-IN-PUBLICATION DATA
Kraus, Robert.
Strudwick / written and illustrated by Robert Kraus.   p. cm.
Summary: Strudwick the sheep dresses up in a wolf costume to trick
the rest of the sheep, but he's the one who is fooled.
ISBN 0-670-85887-0
[1. Costume—Fiction. 2. Sheep—Fiction. 3. Wolves—Fiction. 4. Humorous stories.]
I. Title. PZ7.K868St 1995 [E]—dc20 94-31911 CIP AC

Printed in China
Set in Optima Bold

For Parker.
For Pamela—
she told me to go for it.

Strudwick lived with his mother and father
in a vine-covered cottage at the edge of Sheep Dip Road.

"Beware of the wolf," said Strudwick's father.
"He would like nothing more than to make lamb chops out of you."

"L-l-lamb chops?" stammered Strudwick.
"You bet," said Strudwick's father.

"Remember,
the wolf
is a master
of disguise.
He may even
be dressed
in sheep's
clothing."

"A wolf in sheep's clothing?" asked Strudwick.
"Yes," said his father. "Watch your back at all times."

Strudwick looked at his father suspiciously.
Could he be . . . ? No, thank goodness, *he*
surely wasn't the wolf in sheep's clothing.

Then Strudwick got an idea! He went to the costume store and rented a wolf suit.

Two can play the disguise game, he thought.

But no one was fooled. A cow kept chewing.

The birds kept singing, and a rabbit laughed.

He tried to scare the other little lambs, but they laughed at him. "Don't try to pull the wool over our eyes!" they bleated.

Strudwick was very sad.

"I can't seem to fool anybody," he said.
"But I bet I could fool my grandpa. He's old
and very nearsighted."

"May I visit Grandpa?" Strudwick asked his mother.

"That's a good idea," said his mother. "He's been
feeling poorly and would enjoy your company. But be
careful that the wolf doesn't gobble you up."

"Don't worry," said Strudwick. "I'll be wearing
my wolf costume."

So his mother packed a basket of goodies for
Grandpa, and Strudwick was on his way.

He had not gone far when he came upon the sly and hungry wolf
(wearing his sheep disguise, no less).

"Oh, please don't eat me, Mr. Wolf," said the wolf in sheep's clothing.
He thinks I'm a wolf, thought Strudwick. *I've fooled him! What fun!*

"Don't worry," he said. "I prefer my mutton aged. There's an old

grandfather sheep who lives alone at the far edge of the woods. I'm going to have him for dinner."

"In that case I'll be on my way," said the sly wolf in sheep's clothing.

"Be careful," said Strudwick. "Other wolves may not be so kind."

The sly wolf whisked off his sheep's clothing and put on a mailman's cap. He hurried off to Grandpa's house, for he too preferred aged mutton. While Strudwick dallied, picking flowers for Grandpa, the sly wolf rapped on Grandpa's front door. "Special delivery for Grampy," he crooned in his special delivery mailman's voice.

Grandpa, being no fool or he wouldn't have lived so long, peeped through the peephole in the door. "The wicked wolf!" he muttered under his breath. "I'll show him what for!"

He quickly slipped into his lion-suit disguise and opened the door.

"RRRRROOAAARRRRR!!!!" roared Grandpa.
"YIPE!" screamed the wolf. "WRONG HOUSE!!!"

He hightailed it into the woods, almost knocking over Strudwick
in his haste.

"He looks familiar," said Strudwick to himself, "but I can't quite place him."

Strudwick hurried on to his grandfather's cottage,
and knocked on the door. A lion answered.
"What have you done with Grandpa?" demanded Strudwick.

"Nothing," said Grandpa, taking off his lion suit.
"I am Grandpa. But please don't eat me, Mr. Wolf."

"I'm not a wolf. I'm your grandson," said Strudwick, zipping off his suit.

"You could have fooled me," said Grandpa.

They had a picnic under a shady tree, and agreed
you can't be too careful when it comes to wolves.